AUNTIE KATUSHKA BROUGHT A HUGE BAG FILLED WITH PRESENTS

Three Stories From
# The Poppy Seed Cakes

by Margery Clark
Pictures by
Maud & Miska Petersham

SCHOLASTIC BOOK SERVICES
NEW YORK · TORONTO · LONDON · AUCKLAND · SYDNEY · TOKYO

Copyright 1924 by Doubleday & Company, Inc. This abridged edition is published by Scholastic Book Services, a division of Scholastic Magazines, Inc., by arrangement with Doubleday & Company, Inc.

1st printing .................................................................................................................................... January 1972

Printed in the U.S.A.

## Stories

## THE POPPY SEED CAKES

NCE upon a time there was a
little boy and his name was
Andrewshek. His mother and his father

brought him from the old country when he was a tiny baby.

Andrewshek had an Auntie Katushka and she came from the old country, too, on Andrewshek's fourth birthday.

Andrewshek's Auntie Katushka came on a large boat. She brought with her a huge bag filled with presents for Andrewshek and his father and his mother. In the huge bag were a fine feather bed and a bright shawl and five pounds of poppy seeds.

The fine feather bed was made from the feathers of her old green goose at home. It was to keep Andrewshek warm when he took a nap.

The bright shawl was for Andrewshek's Auntie Katushka to wear when

AUNTIE KATUSHKA STARTING HOME FROM THE MARKET

she went to market.

The five pounds of poppy seeds were to sprinkle on little cakes which Andrewshek's Auntie Katushka made every Saturday for Andrewshek.

One lovely Saturday morning Andrewshek's Auntie Katushka took some butter and some sugar and some flour and some milk and seven eggs and she rolled out some nice little cakes. Then she sprinkled each cake with some of the poppy seeds which she had brought from the old country.

While the nice little cakes were baking, she spread out the fine feather bed on top of the big bed, for Andrewshek to take his nap. Andrewshek did not like to take a nap.

SHE SPRINKLED EACH CAKE WITH POPPY SEEDS

Andrewshek loved to bounce up and down and up and down on his fine feather bed.

Andrewshek's Auntie Katushka took the nice little cakes out of the oven and put them on the table to cool; then she put on her bright shawl to go to market. "Andrewshek," she said, "please watch these cakes while you rest on your fine feather bed.   Be sure that the kitten and the dog do not go near them."

"Yes, indeed!   I will watch the nice little cakes," said Andrewshek.   "And I will be sure that the kitten and the dog do not touch them."   But all Andrewshek really did was to bounce up and down and up and down on the fine feather bed.

"Andrewshek!" said Andrewshek's Auntie Katushka, "how can you watch the poppy seed cakes when all you do is to bounce up and down and up and down on the fine feather bed?" Then Andrewshek's Auntie Katushka, in her bright shawl, hurried off to market.

But Andrewshek kept bouncing up and down and up and down on the fine

BOUNCING UP IN THE AIR FOR THE NINTH TIME

feather bed and paid no attention to the little cakes sprinkled with poppy seeds.

Just as Andrewshek was bouncing up in the air for the ninth time, he heard a queer noise that sounded like "Hs-s-s-s-sss," at the front door of his house.

"Oh, what a queer noise!" cried Andrewshek. He jumped down off the fine feather bed and opened the front door. There stood a great green goose as big as Andrewshek himself. The goose was very cross and was scolding as fast as he could. He was wagging his head and was opening and closing his long red beak.

"What do you want?" said Andrewshek. "What are you scolding about?"

"I want all the goose feathers from

your fine feather bed," quacked the big green goose. "They are mine."

"They are not yours," said Andrewshek. "My Auntie Katushka brought them with her from the old country in a huge bag."

"They are mine," quacked the big green goose. He waddled over to the fine feather bed and tugged at it with

THE GREEN GOOSE TUGGED AT THE FINE FEATHER BED

his long red beak.

"Stop, Green Goose!" said Andrew-shek, "and I will give you one of Auntie Katushka's poppy seed cakes."

"A poppy seed cake!" the green goose quacked in delight. "I love nice little poppy seed cakes! Give me one and you shall have your feather bed."

But one poppy seed cake could not

satisfy the greedy green goose.

"Give me another!" Andrewshek gave the green goose another poppy seed cake.

"Give me another!" the big green goose hissed and frightened Andrewshek nearly out of his wits.

Andrewshek gave him another and and another and another till all the poppy seed cakes were gone.

Just as the last poppy seed cake disappeared down the long neck of the green goose, Andrewshek's Auntie Katushka appeared at the door, in her bright shawl. "Boo! hoo!" cried Andrewshek. "See! that naughty green goose has eaten all the poppy seed cakes."

"What? All my nice little poppy

seed cakes?" cried Andrewshek's Auntie
Katushka. "The naughty goose!"

The greedy goose tugged at the fine
feather bed again with his long red
beak and started to drag it to the door.
Andrewshek's Auntie Katushka ran after
the green goose and just then there was
a dreadful explosion. The greedy goose
who had stuffed himself with poppy seed

cakes had burst and his feathers flew all over the room.

"Well! well!" said Andrewshek's Auntie Katushka, as she gathered up the pieces of the big green goose. "We soon shall have two fine feather pillows for your fine feather bed."

# THE WHITE GOAT

ONE fine Saturday morning Andrewshek's Auntie Katushka said, "Andrewshek, I must go to market and buy a goat."

Andrewshek was playing in the garden. He had pulled out some of the feathers from his fine feather bed and had put them in his hair. He looked very funny.

As Andrewshek's Auntie Katushka went out of the gate to go to market, Andrewshek said, "May I go with you, Auntie Katushka?"

"No, Andrewshek!" said his Auntie Katushka. "You must stay at home. Please watch to see that the dog does not open the gate and let the chickens and the cat run out into the road."

"Yes, indeed, I will watch to see that the dog does not open the gate. And I will be sure that the chickens and the cat do not run out into the road."

Then Auntie Katushka, in her bright shawl, hurried off to market. But all Andrewshek really did was to swing backward and forward and backward and forward on the dark green gate.

Andrewshek loved to swing backward and forward on the gate just as much as he loved to bounce up and down on his fine feather bed.

At the market Auntie Katushka saw a white goat. The white goat had a long beard and a short tail. "That is just the goat I want!" said Auntie Katushka.

"White Goat!" said Auntie Katushka. "I am going to take you home with me to Andrewshek."

"Who is Andrewshek?" said the goat.

"Andrewshek is a little boy who lives across the tracks and up the hill, in a little house with a dark green gate. Andrewshek loves to swing backward and forward and backward and forward on the dark green gate."

"I would not be surprised if Andrewshek was swinging backward and forward on the green gate now," said the

ALL ANDREWSHEK DID WAS TO SWING BACKWARD AND FORWARD
AND BACKWARD AND FORWARD

goat to herself. "I think I'll run ahead and see."

She galloped off.

"Stop, White Goat!" cried Auntie Katushka. "Stop!"

But the goat did not stop. She ran faster and faster, across the tracks and up the hill until she came to the little house with the dark green gate. Andrewshek was swinging backward and forward and backward and forward on the dark green gate. The chickens and the cat had long before run out into the road.

"How do you do, Andrewshek?" said the white goat.

"How do you do, White Goat?" said Andrewshek. "Where are you going?"

"HOW DO YOU DO, ANDREWSHEK?"

"No further!" said the white goat. "I belong to your Auntie Katushka."

"Where is my Auntie Katushka?" said Andrewshek.

"I ran away from her, across the tracks and up the hill; and here I am!" said the goat.

"Won't Auntie Katushka be surprised when she sees you here!" said Andrewshek.

"I think I will hide!" said the white goat. She ran behind the little house.

Andrewshek's Auntie Katushka, in her bright shawl, came hurrying up the hill.

"Andrewshek, I bought a sweet white goat at the market, to give us milk for our poppy seed cakes. She ran away and so we cannot have any poppy seed cakes to-day. I wonder how we can find her!"

"Ha! ha! ha!" the sweet white goat called out. She had climbed to the top of the roof where she could look down on Andrewshek and Auntie Katushka.

"Come down from the roof, you naughty White Goat!" said Auntie Katushka.

The goat shook her head.

"Please come down!" said Andrewshek. "And I will give you a big poppy seed cake."

"I do not like poppy seed cakes," said the naughty white goat.

"What shall we do?" said Andrewshek.

Andrewshek's Auntie Katushka

"I DO NOT LIKE POPPY SEED CAKES," SAID THE NAUGHTY WHITE GOAT

went into the house and took off her bright shawl. She put on her apron.

She washed some turnips and some parsnips, two onions and four carrots for the soup. Then she cut the green tops from the vegetables. She put the green tops in a basket. "Goats love fresh green tops," she said to Andrewshek, as she put the basket on the back porch by the door.   She left the door wide open.

The naughty white goat was peeping over the roof to see what she could see.  She saw the green tops in the basket by the kitchen door.  Immediately she felt very hungry.  She clambered down from the roof. She stole up to the basket.

"Well! well!" laughed Andrewshek's

Auntie Katushka, as she slipped a halter around the white goat's neck. "We soon shall have plenty of milk for our poppy seed cakes."

## THE PICNIC BASKET

NE cool summer morning Andrewshek's Auntie Katushka
said, "Andrewshek, I think I will put
some sandwiches and some cottage

cheese and some poppy seed cakes and two eggs in our picnic basket.  Then we will go to the park and eat our lunch there, near the water."

"May I go with you, Auntie Katush-ka?" said Andrewshek.

"Of course you may go to the park with me," said Auntie Katushka.  "But first we have a great many things to do, before we can start to the park.  I must go into the garden and catch the white goat.  I will tie her up so she will not run away.  Please find the kitten, Andrewshek, and put her in the cellar, so she will not worry the chickens while we are gone."

"Yes, indeed, I will find the kitten and put her in the cellar," said Andrewshek, "so she will not worry the chickens while we are gone."

But all Andrewshek really did was to lift up the red and white napkin which Auntie Katushka had laid over the picnic basket and look at the eggs and the poppy seed cakes and touch the sandwiches and taste the cottage cheese.

The goat was not easy to catch. The

THE GOAT WAS NOT EASY TO CATCH

goat wanted to go to the park, too.   She galloped round and round the garden.

At last Auntie Katushka caught her and tied her firmly to a post.

Then Auntie Katushka went into the house to get Andrewshek and the lunch basket. She saw Andrewshek peeping under the red and white napkin and tasting the cottage cheese.   He had forgotten all about the kitten.

The kitten was nowhere to be found. "I think she must be paying a visit to the Mouse family," said Auntie Katushka.

Then Auntie Katushka put on her bright shawl and took her umbrella with the long crooked handle under one arm. Then she picked up the lunch basket with the red and white napkin on top and she and Andrewshek started for the park.

They went down the hill and across the tracks and past the market and down a long street until they came to the park by the water.

Andrewshek sat down on the grass beside a little stream. Andrewshek's Auntie Katushka laid her umbrella with the long crooked handle and the basket of lunch on the grass beside Andrew-shek.

"Andrewshek," said Auntie Katush-ka, "I must go to the spring and get some water for us to drink. Please watch the basket with the eggs and the sandwiches and poppy seed cakes and cottage cheese while I am gone."

"Yes, indeed, I will watch the basket of lunch," said Andrewshek.

But what Andrewshek really did was to say to himself, "I would like to take off my shoes and my stockings and wade in the little stream. I believe I will!"

Andrewshek took off his shoes and his stockings and went wading in the little stream.

ANDREWSHEK SAT DOWN ON THE GRASS

A big white swan came floating calmly down the stream. He saw the picnic basket lying on the grass. He stopped and stretched and stretched his long neck, till he could touch the basket. "Honk! honk! honk!" said he. "I wonder what is under the red and white napkin."

The big white swan lifted the napkin

with his red bill and looked in the basket. "Oh, oh, oh! Won't Mother Swan be pleased with this nice lunch!" said he. "Sandwich bread makes fine food for baby swans."

He picked up the basket in his strong red bill and floated it ahead of him down the stream.

Andrewshek could not wade after

the big white swan.  The water was too deep.

"Stop! stop! White Swan!" cried Andrewshek.  "That is my Auntie Katushka's picnic basket and it has our lunch in it.  Please put it back on the grass."

"No, indeed!  I will not put the basket back," honked the big white

ANDREWSHEK COULD NOT WADE AFTER THE BIG WHITE SWAN

swan. "Sandwich bread makes fine food for baby swans and I have ten baby swans to feed."

The big white swan gave the picnic basket a little push with his red bill. The basket floated on down the little stream. The big white swan floated calmly behind it.

Just then Andrewshek's Auntie Katushka came hurrying up with the spring water.  She saw the big white swan floating down the stream, with the lunch basket floating ahead of him.

Andrewshek stood in the middle of the stream, crying.

Auntie Katushka picked up her umbrella with the long crooked handle. Auntie Katushka ran along the shore until she overtook the big white swan, with the lunch basket floating ahead of him.

She caught the handle of the picnic basket in the crook of her long handled umbrella. She drew the basket safely to shore.

"Well! well!" said Auntie Katushka, as she spread the red and white napkin on the grass, and laid the sandwiches and the poppy seed cakes and the cottage cheese and the eggs upon it. "It always pays to carry an umbrella to a picnic."